Dedicated to all those
who would like to be lucky

Copyright © 1986 Nord-Süd Verlag, Mönchaltorf, Switzerland
First published in Switzerland under the title Hans im Glück
English text copyright © 1986 Jock Curle
Copyright English language edition under the imprint
North-South Books © 1986 Rada Matija AG, Staefa, Switzerland

First published in the United States, Great Britain, Canada,
Australia and New Zealand in 1986 by North-South Books, an
imprint of Rada Matija AG.

Distributed in the United States by
Henry Holt and Company, 383 Madison Avenue
New York, New York 10017.
Library of Congress Cataloging in Publication Data

Hans im Glück. English.
  Lucky Hans.

  Translation of: Hans im Glück.
  Summary: When his seven years' wages in gold prove too
heavy to carry easily, Hans trades the lump of gold for
one thing after another until he arrives home empty-
handed, but convinced he is a lucky man to be unfret-
tered with encumbrances.
  [1. Fairy tales.   2. Folklore--Germany]   I. Grimm,
Wilhelm, 1786–1859.   II. Grimm, Jacob, 1785–1863.
III. Sopko, Eugen, ill.   IV. Title.
PZ8.L965   1986   398.2'1'0943   [E]   86-2520

ISBN 0-8050-0009-7

Distributed in Great Britain by
Blackie and Son Ltd, 7 Leicester Place,
London WC 2H 7BP.
British Library Cataloguing in Publication Data

Grimm, Jacob
  Lucky Hans.
  1. Tales —— Germany
  I. Title   II. Grimm, Wilhelm   III. Sopko,
  Eugen   IV. Curle, Jock
  398.2'1'0943   PZ8.1

ISBN 0-200-72889-X

Distributed in Canada by
Douglas & McIntyre Ltd., Toronto.
Canadian Cataloguing in Publication Data available in
Marc Record from National Library of Canada.
ISBN 0 88894 780 1

Distributed in Australia and New Zealand by
Buttercup Books Pty. Ltd., Melbourne.
ISBN 0 949447 30 7

Printed in Germany

Lucky Hans

a Fairy Tale by
Jacob and Wilhelm Grimm
retold by Jock Curle

illustrated by
EUGEN SOPKO

North-South Books
New York   London   Toronto   Melbourne

When Hans had served his master faithfully for seven years, he began to feel homesick. "Give me my wages," he said, "and I shall go back to my mother."

"You have worked well," said his master. "Here is your reward," and he gave Hans a lump of gold as big as his head.

Hans set off for home and soon met a man on a fine horse.

"How pleasant it would be," he said, "to ride at ease like that. No more holes in my shoes; no more sore feet. Yet, instead of riding, I've got this great lump of gold to carry."

"Well, we can easily arrange things better than that," said the man. "You give me your gold and I shall give you my horse."

Hans was delighted with his horse, until suddenly it
kicked up its heels and threw him to the ground.

Luckily a farmer leading a cow caught the horse and brought it back to him.

"I'll never get on that creature's back again," said Hans. "It's more than my life is worth. Now, with a cow like yours, I could walk quietly behind her, and have milk, butter and cheese whenever I felt like it."

"If you will give me your horse, I will give you my cow with pleasure," said the farmer.

Hans quickly agreed.

As Hans drove his cow down lanes and through meadows, he thought how lucky he was. "All I need," he said to himself, "is a piece of bread. The cow will provide me with butter and cheese to put on it, and a drink of milk to wash it down."

When he came to an inn, Hans spent the last of his money on a glass of beer and ate the last of the food he had brought with him.

Afterwards, Hans set off across a wide heath. The day was hot, and soon he felt thirsty again. He tried to milk his cow into his hat as he had no pail. But his clumsy hands only hurt the cow, and with a sharp kick to his head, she sent him flying.

Luckily a butcher came by with a pig in a wheel-barrow. "You'll get no milk out of that cow," he said. "She's too old for milk and too stringy for beef."

"If only I had a pig like yours!" said Hans. "At least then I could make myself some sausages."

"Well," said the butcher, "just to please you, I'm prepared to do a swop."

So the butcher took the cow and went on his way.

"I'm not going to wheel you in the barrow," said Hans to the pig, "that's too much like work." So he tied a string to its leg, tipped it out on the ground, and off they went.

Before long Hans met a man carrying a goose under his arm. They got talking and Hans told him his story.

"My friend," said the man, "you have certainly struck some wonderful bargains. Unfortunately, I think your luck has run out with that pig."

"Why do you say that?" asked Hans.

"In the village for which you are heading," said the man, "the mayor was robbed of a prize pig this morning. I very much fear this is it."

"What can I do?" said Hans.

"Probably I shall lose by it," answered the man. "Still, to help a friend in need, I will take the pig off you, and you can have my fine goose in exchange."

Hans thanked the man warmly and they set off on their separate ways. "I've done well out of that," thought Hans. "The goose will roast splendidly, I shall have lots of goose grease, and the feathers will make a wonderfully soft pillow. How pleased my mother will be."

As he came to the last village before reaching home, he met a knife-grinder working away at the side of the road. His wheel spun and sparks flew. Hans thought this would be a fine job.

The knife-grinder asked Hans where he had got the goose, and Hans told him his story.

"You've done very well, so far," said the knife-grinder. "However, what you really need is a steady job that will bring you money every day. You should be a knife-grinder like me. I tell you what," he went on, "why don't you give me that goose, and I'll let you have my old grind-stone. It's a bit worn, but there's plenty of life in it yet." The knife-grinder bent down and picked up a large stone from the ground. "Look," he said, "I'll give you this stone as well for luck."

So Hans gave the knife-grinder his goose, picked up the old grindstone and went on his way. "What a lucky fellow I am," he thought. "Everything turns out well for me."

But soon he began to feel tired. He had had no food since daybreak and the grindstone was heavy.

At last he came to a well and decided to rest for a while.

Hans laid his grindstone on the edge of the well and started to draw himself some water. However, as he lowered the bucket into the water, it swung round and knocked the grindstone into the well.

"Thank goodness," cried Hans, laughing and clapping his hands. "That great heavy grindstone was the last of my troubles and heaven has taken it away. What a lucky fellow I am, to be sure. Now I am free to run home and greet my mother without a single thing in the world to bother me."